BUILD YOUR HARRY POTTER MINIFIGURE!

1

2

SCHOOL OF MAGIC

Future witches and wizards who have been accepted to Hogwarts receive a letter on their eleventh birthdays.

Help this owl deliver Harry's Hogwarts letter, avoiding Aunt Petunia and Uncle Vernon on the way.

START

FINISH

Did you know . . .?

A Hogwarts letter will always find its addressee. Even if that person is away from home!

Answer on page 94.

In Diagon Alley, students can buy everything for their classes, including: wands, potion ingredients, textbooks, and broomsticks.

Has Harry managed to get everything he needs? Check off the items you see in the picture.

Answers on page 94.

The Hogwarts Express departs on September 1 at 11:00 a.m. from Platform 9¾ at King's Cross Station.

To get to Platform 9¾, enter the wall between platforms 9 and 10. Find and circle 10 differences in the pictures below.

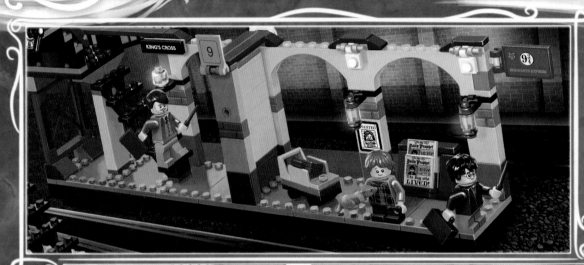

Did you know . . .?

Dobby, the house-elf, once closed the passage to Platform 9¾ right under Harry's and Ron's noses!

Answers on page 94.

The Hogwarts Express journey is really long, so the students don't reach school until the evening.

The Hogwarts Express is just about to appear! Connect each set of colored dots one by one to see what this train looks like.

Answer on page 94.

Harry met his best friends, Ron and Hermione, on the way to Hogwarts. Since then, they have become almost inseparable!

Harry, Ron, and Hermione have had a lot of adventures together. Match the torn pictures halves by drawing lines to connect them.

Did you know . . .?

Ron is from a wizarding family. He has five brothers and a sister. Hermione is an only child and her parents do not have any magical abilities.

Answers on page 94.

Hogwarts students get along very well. But there are some exceptions, such as Harry and Draco!

Harry and Draco compete anytime, anywhere! Enter the correct numbers in the missing portraits as the two go head-to-head in dominoes.

Answers on page 94.

Albus Dumbledore is a powerful wizard and one of the most famous headmasters in the history of Hogwarts!

Follow the color code to find the Chocolate Frog card that Professor Dumbledore was looking for.

START

Did you know . . .?

Professor Dumbledore once came across a vomit-flavored Bertie Bott's Every Flavor Bean.

 Answer on page 94.

The Hogwarts Headmaster's office is full of magical surprises. Talking portraits, the Pensieve, and so much more!

Professor Dumbledore's office is also home to Fawkes—a phoenix that transforms. Color in Fawkes using the code of colored dots below.

Answer on page 94.

At Hogwarts, students are placed in one of four houses: Gryffindor, Slytherin, Ravenclaw, or Hufflepuff.

Did you know . . .?

Each Hogwarts house has its own crest, Head of House, prefect, ghost, Quidditch team, and common room.

TEST YOURSELF

Find out which Hogwarts house you fit in best.

1 Choose a portrait to hang in your room.

A  B  C  D

2 Which animal do you prefer?

A  B  C  D

3 Pick a fun combination of colors.

A   B   C   D

4 Choose who you'd share your school desk with.

A   B   C   D

5 Your favorite school subject would be:

A   B   C   D

Transfiguration   Herbology   Charms   Potions

A, B, C, or maybe D? Count your answers
and discover the house for you!

A Gryffindor   B Hufflepuff   C Ravenclaw   D Slytherin

The Sorting Ceremony begins every school year at Hogwarts. Students starting their education are sorted into houses.

The Sorting Hat selects houses for Hogwarts students. Find and circle the magic hat that is different from the others!

Did you know . . .?

The Sorting Hat wanted to place Harry in Slytherin, but at his request, it put him in Gryffindor.

Answer on page 94.

After the headmaster's speech and important announcements, the Great Feast begins.

The food magically appears in front of the students! Look at the Feast and draw the treats that repeat on the neighboring tables.

Each Hogwarts house has a professor who is in charge of the students.

Untangle the lines and match the professor to their house crest by writing the correct letters in the blank spaces below!

A
Filius Flitwick

B
Minerva McGonagall

C
Pomona Sprout

D
Severus Snape

Head of Ravenclaw House

Head of Gryffindor House

Head of Slytherin House

Head of Hufflepuff House

Students earn points for correct answers in class and good behavior. The house with the most points receives the House Cup!

Would you earn house points for this task? Add up the symbol values for each picture and circle the one where you can score the most points.

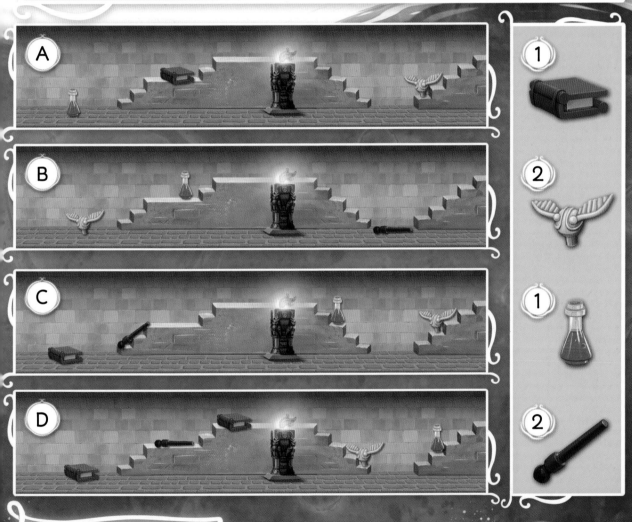

Did you know . . .?

The House Cup winner is unpredictable. Once Slytherin was set to win, but Gryffindor earned extra points at the last minute!

Answer on page 94.

The prefects take first-year students around the school and tell them about the most important school rules.

Students must say a secret password to enter their house. Find the cloud shape that is identical to Neville's to remind him of the Gryffindor password.

GODRIC GRYFFINDOR

?

SHERBET LEMON

MERLIN'S BEARD

CAPUT DRACONIS

Did you know . . .?

The stairs at Hogwarts move and can change their path, even when you're walking on them!

Answer on page 94.

Every house at Hogwarts has a common room. This is where students spend their time studying, talking, or playing their favorite magical games.

Oops! The portrait of Godric Gryffindor is a bit dusty. Dust it off by writing the numbers of the fragments in the grayed-out boxes.

Hogwarts students begin each day with breakfast served in the Great Hall. This is where they eat all of their meals.

When it's dark, the Great Hall is lit by floating candles. Color the flames to make the candles match on either side of Harry.

Did you know . . .?

The ceiling in the Great Hall is enchanted to look like the night sky!

Answers on page 94.

Every morning, owls bring students letters, all kinds of packages, and the latest issue of *the Daily Prophet*.

Draw straight lines to connect the identical owls. The item not crossed by any of the lines is a package for one of the students.

Gryffindor's Head of House, Minerva McGonagall, is an accomplished witch who has the ability to transfigure into a cat at any time.

Professor McGonagall also teaches . . . dance classes! To find the professor's dance partner, circle the portrait that appears only once.

Did you know . . .?

Professor McGonagall is a big fan of Quidditch. She was the one who discovered Harry's talent and invited him to join the Gryffindor Quidditch team.

Answer on page 94.

Professor McGonagall teaches Transfiguration—the ability to change the appearance of objects, animals, and even people.

Fill in the correct letters underneath each creature to discover the spell that turns animals into water cups.

Answer on page 94.

The Head of Slytherin, Severus Snape, taught Potions for years before becoming the Defense Against the Dark Arts teacher.

A black robe and a grumpy expression are some of Severus Snape's defining features. Circle the set with five different poses of the professor.

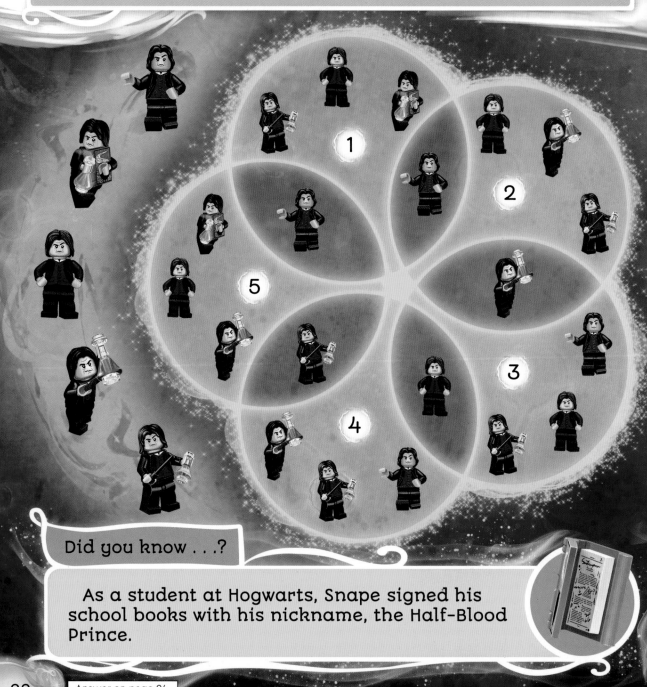

Did you know . . .?

As a student at Hogwarts, Snape signed his school books with his nickname, the Half-Blood Prince.

Answer on page 94.

During Potions classes, students must be careful and organized. A drop of the wrong ingredient can cause . . . a huge BOOM!

There should be order in the Potions Classroom. Color the empty bottles so that they're arranged in the same order on each shelf.

Argus Filch has no magical abilities, but he is a true Hogwarts legend! He's infamous for catching rule breakers red-handed.

At night, Filch goes on patrol. Find out where by completing each picture with the matching puzzle piece.

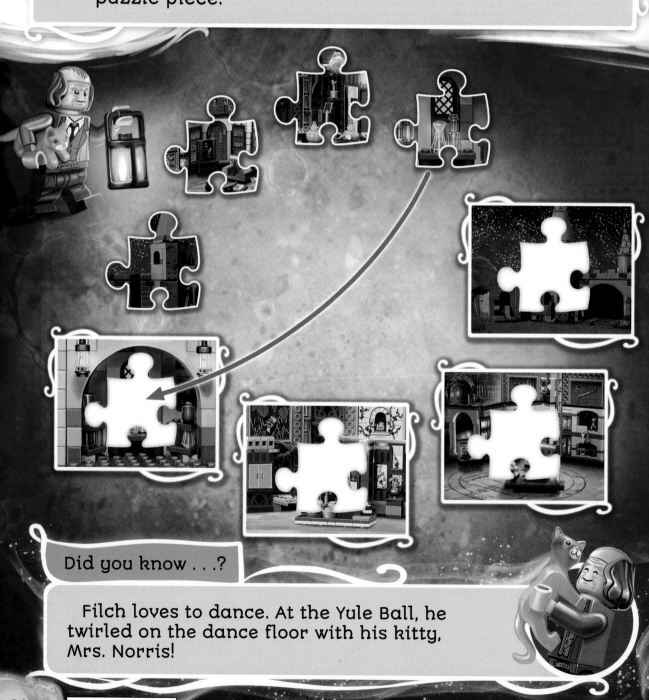

Did you know . . .?

Filch loves to dance. At the Yule Ball, he twirled on the dance floor with his kitty, Mrs. Norris!

Answers on page 94.

This cat is not only Filch's animal companion, but she's also his assistant. She wanders the school corridors and meows whenever she sees students breaking the rules!

Mrs. Norris seems to be in several places at once. Help the friends get back to Gryffindor Tower without running into Filch's cat.

START

FINISH

Answer on page 94.

During Harry's first year at Hogwarts, a huge three-headed dog named Fluffy lived on the third floor of the castle.

Fluffy was guarding the Sorcerer's Stone. Take a look and find the dangerous guardian that is different from the others.

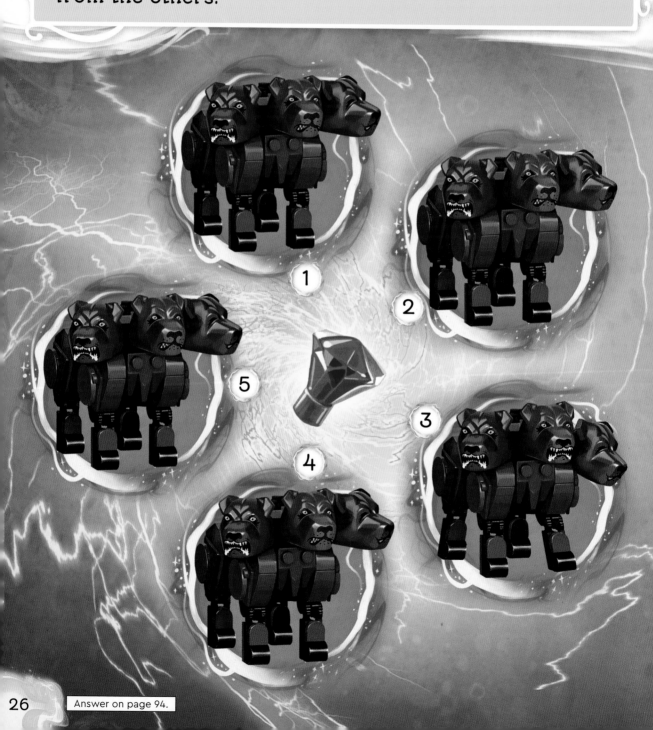

Answer on page 94.

It's better not to visit one of the girls' bathrooms! Unless you want to meet Moaning Myrtle—a ghost who cries all the time.

Moaning Myrtle loves to hide in her stall! Lead her to this hiding place by following the order of the tiles in the key below.

KEY

START

FINISH

Did you know . . .?

Moaning Myrtle is the ghost of Myrtle Warren, a former Hogwarts student who was in Ravenclaw.

Answer on page 94.

A long time ago, Salazar Slytherin created a secret chamber beneath the castle to keep a dangerous creature—the Basilisk.

Help Harry open the magic door to the Chamber of Secrets! Write the letters of the pieces in the correct spaces below.

Did you know . . .?

A huge snake with a deadly gaze, the Basilisk has a reflection that will petrify anyone who sees it.

Answers on page 94.

For his first Christmas at Hogwarts, Harry was given an Invisibility Cloak, which is a robe that can make anyone who wears it invisible.

Harry can move around the school undetected by Filch. Follow the clues below and circle the box where he is hiding this time.

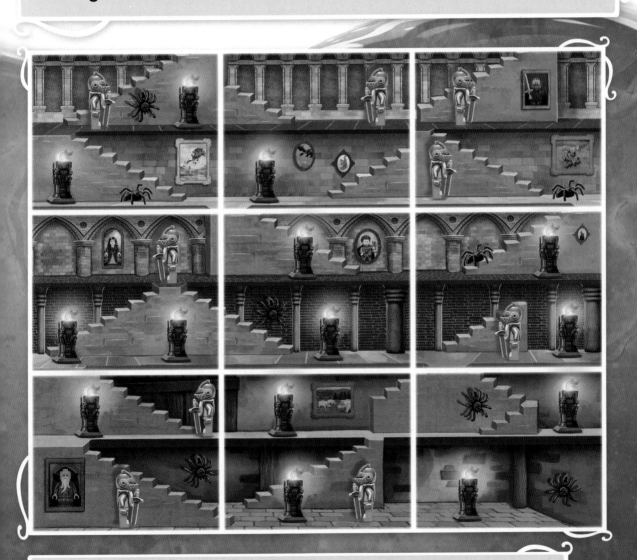

Harry can be found in the box:

- with pictures on the wall
- lit by a single torch
- with a knight's armor
- with a staircase of six steps

This amazing map shows everyone who is at Hogwarts. However, it reveals its secrets only to those who say, "I solemnly swear that I am up to no good."

The Marauder's Map was created by Moony, Padfoot, Prongs, and Wormtail. Match the shadows to the characters by writing the numbers in the spaces below and find out who these nicknames belong to.

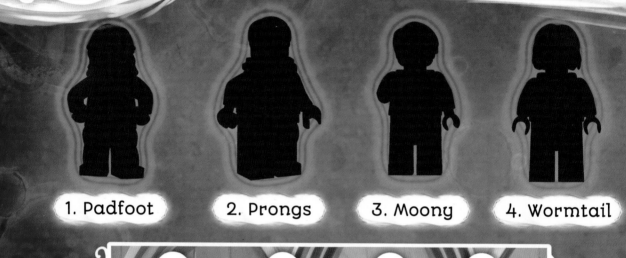

1. Padfoot   2. Prongs   3. Moony   4. Wormtail

Did you know . . .?

For years, the map was hidden in Filch's office. That's where Ron's twin brothers, Fred and George, found it.

The Marauder's Map shows seven secret passages leading from Hogwarts to various places around the castle and to Hogsmeade.

One secret passage leads to Honeydukes sweet shop. Help Harry get there by connecting the fragments to create a tunnel to the shop.

START

FINISH

Answer on page 95.

Rolanda Hooch is a witch who teaches flying lessons at Hogwarts. She is also a referee at school Quidditch matches.

What a rush! Take a look at Madam Hooch flying on her broomstick. Then write the correct numbers in the boxes below to match the mixed-up fragments to the picture.

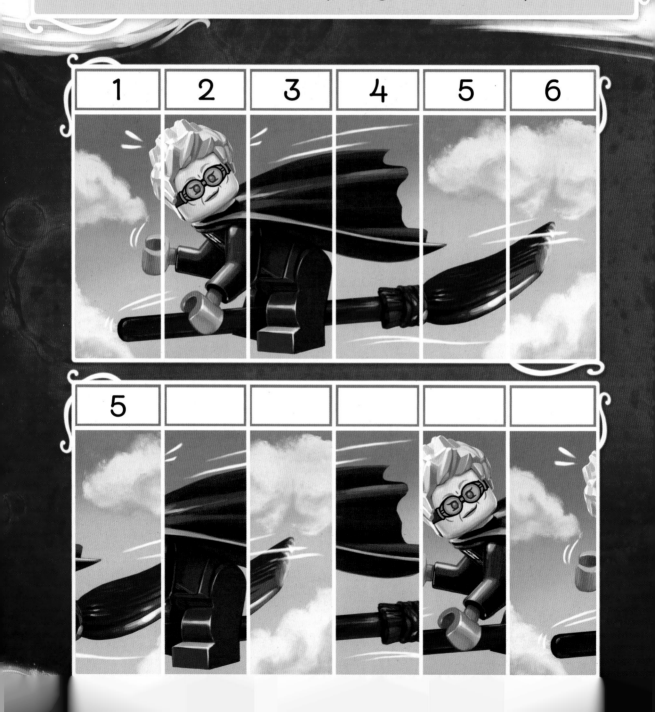

All Hogwarts students learn to fly a broom during their first year. These classes take place in front of the castle.

The first flying lesson is always very exciting. See for yourself and mark whether the fragments appear in the large picture below.

Did you know . . .?

Flying class is one of the few subjects that Hermione struggles with.

Each house's Quidditch team captain selects the team players during training at the beginning of the year.

The Gryffindor team needs a new Keeper. Find him by circling the portrait sets below and selecting the player remaining.

Did you know . . .?

Years ago, James Potter (Harry's dad) was the Gryffindor Quidditch team's Seeker.

Answers on page 95.

During Quidditch trainings, practice matches are often held to prepare players for real games.

Match the players performing identical stunts. The player without a pair is the captain of the Gryffindor team!

Answers on page 95.

Quidditch teams compete against each other throughout the school year. When school ends, the team with the most points is awarded the Quidditch Cup.

Here is the schedule of school games. Identify the crests by the shapes and write the first letters of the house names on them—this way you will find out who won each game!

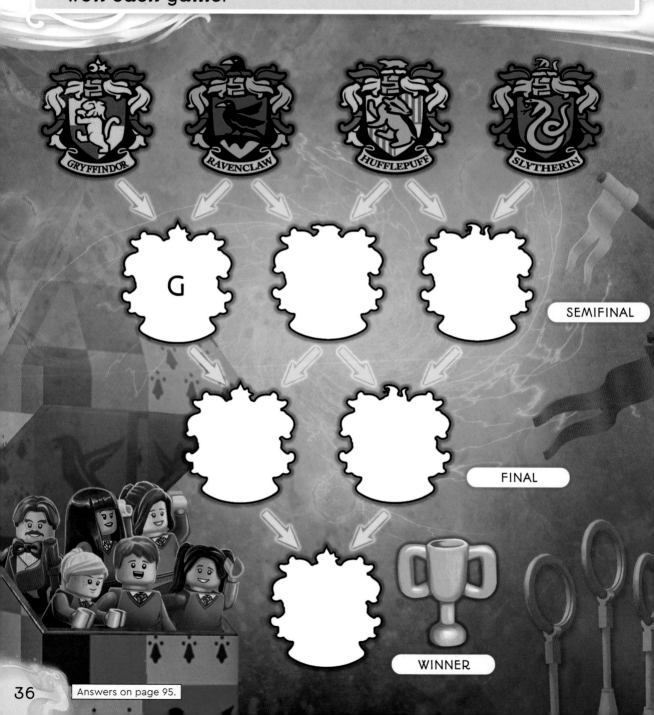

GRYFFINDOR

RAVENCLAW

HUFFLEPUFF

SLYTHERIN

G

SEMIFINAL

FINAL

WINNER

Answers on page 95.

During the school games, the stands are always full of fans. The matches are attended by the students and the teachers.

Quidditch fans have banners, flags, scarves, and hats in the colors of their favorite team. Identify the student in the Gryffindor lion costume and check off her picture.

Did you know . . .?

Some fans also use magic binoculars during Quidditch matches to watch the action up close!

Answer on page 95.

Quidditch is one of the most popular sports in the wizarding world!

TEST YOUR KNOWLEDGE

Complete the sentences to find out what kind of Quidditch fan you would be.

1

The Quidditch team consists of _____ players.

Hint: A number greater than six but less than eight.

1. Five
2. Six
3. Seven
4. Eight

2

A magic ball with wings is named_____.

Hint: Its color is hidden in its name.

1. A Bludger
2. A Quaffle
3. A Golden Snitch
4. A Remembrall

3

Quidditch matches take place _____.

Hint: You can breathe fresh air there.

1. In the open air
2. Underground
3. Indoor
4. Underwater

4

For catching the Golden Snitch, the team scores _____ points.

Hint: The largest of the given numbers.

1. Ten
2. Fifty
3. One hundred
4. One hundred and fifty

5

The most important Quidditch competition is _____.

Hint: A global event.

1. Hogwarts Quidditch Cup
2. World Cup
3. Halloween
4. The Triwizard Tournament

Go to page 95 to check your answers and see what kind of a fan you could be.

1–2 correct answers	THE YAWNING ONE—the game would quickly bore you.

3–4 correct answers	THE OBSERVING ONE—you would keep a close eye on what is happening on the pitch.

5 correct answers	THE EXCITING ONE—you would jump for joy after every successful play your team makes.

Answers on page 95.

Filius Flitwick is the Head of Ravenclaw House and the teacher of Charms, one of the most important Hogwarts subjects.

Professor Flitwick is checking which students have already arrived at Hogwarts. Circle the student who is missing in each picture.

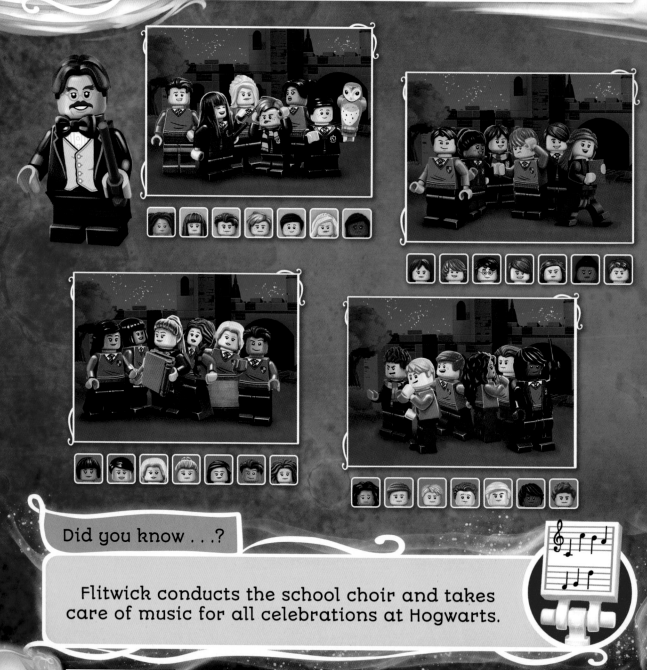

Did you know . . .?

Flitwick conducts the school choir and takes care of music for all celebrations at Hogwarts.

Answers on page 95.

Students attend Charms from their first year at Hogwarts. This is where they learn the basics of magic.

Oops! Seamus caused a small explosion. Get rid of the smoke and match the picture fragments by filling in the correct numbers.

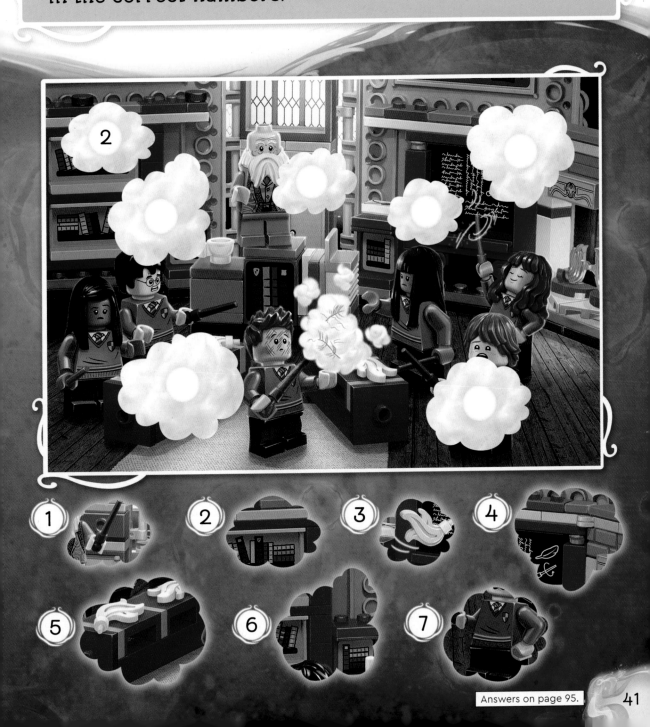

Answers on page 95.

This huge library is full of magic books. Some of them can even put themselves on the shelves!

Hermione loves being in the school library. Join her and number the stacks of magic books from the shortest to the tallest one.

1

Answers on page 95.

The books at Hogwarts are just like the ones at Muggle schools. But there are exceptional textbooks, such as *The Monster Book of Monsters*.

Warning! *The Monster Book of Monsters* can bite! Help Neville choose an escape route below—the numbers show how many books you'll need to skip.

START

X – 2 – 3 – 4 – 1 – 4 – 2 – 4

X – 2 – 3 – 4 – 1 – 3 – 4 – 2

X – 2 – 3 – 4 – 1 – 3 – 2 – 4

1

FINISH

Did you know . . . ?

The only way to open *The Monster Book of Monsters* without being bitten is to pet this magical book's spine.

Answer on page 95.

The Head of Hufflepuff, Pomona Sprout, teaches Herbology—the science of plants with magical properties.

Professor Sprout has her own greenhouse where she grows Mandrakes. Arrange and divide them into groups of four different seedlings.

Answers on page 95.

Protective clothing is required during Herbology because students sometimes encounter dangerous plants.

Mark the fragments below that appear in the picture of Herbology class.

Did you know . . .?

Neville fainted in class when he heard a Mandrake's cry. Despite this incident, Herbology is his favorite subject.

Answers on page 95.

Hogwarts has a new Defense Against the Dark Arts teacher almost every year. Harry has been taught by six different professors!

Put check marks above the teachers who have a matching outline. The one without an outline has never taught Defense Against the Dark Arts.

Did you know . . .?

Professor Snape was able to fulfill his dream of becoming the Defense Against the Dark Arts teacher when Professor Slughorn returned to Hogwarts to teach Potions again.

 Answers on page 95.

Students learn how to defend themselves against dark powers and terrifying magical creatures.

Today's topic is Cornish pixies. Circle the three groups shown below in the swarm that is attacking Neville.

Answers on page 95.

Some Defense Against the Dark Arts teachers like teaching skills. Others like teaching theory from thick textbooks.

One professor had the students copy the pages from the textbook. Follow the arrow pattern that matches the one shown in the purple box below to find out who it was.

Answer on page 95.

Quirinus Quirrell was the first Defense Against the Dark Arts teacher Harry met. His turban hid a dark secret.

Under Professor Quirrell's turban was the evil wizard Lord Voldemort. Color his picture according to the colored dots below.

Did you know . . .?

In the Mirror of Erised—the magic mirror showing one's greatest desires—Professor Quirrell saw himself holding the Sorcerer's Stone.

Every wizard and witch must cast spells for each situation and say the magic words carefully.

Did you know . . .?

Some wizards use nonverbal spells, which are spells that are cast without words.

TEST YOUR KNOWLEDGE

Take the quiz and see how you would handle magic.

1

Oculus Reparo **charm:**

Hint: It is useful for wizards with a visual impairment.

1. Repairs broken glasses
2. Allows one to be invisible
3. Ties a tie

2

Lumos **charm:**

Hint: Valuable after sunset.

1. Turns off all the lights
2. Illuminates every darkness
3. Freezes everything around

3

Alohomora **charm:**

Hint: It will help anyone who lost their keys.

1. Causes a small explosion
2. Opens every door
3. Allows one to read minds

4

Engorgio charm:

Hint: It will be helpful for a giant.

1. Changes color
2. Lifts any object
3. Enlarges everything

5

Diminuendo charm:

Hint: Makes it possible to fit a lot of stuff in a small purse.

1. Shrinks any object
2. Duplicates any object
3. Breaks any object

Go to page 95 to check your answers and see what kind of wizard you would be:

1–2 correct answers

A wizard who could use some lessons in spell matching.

3–4 correct answers

A wizard who can deal with most magical troubles.

5 correct answers

A wizard who can always find the right spell for every situation.

Meet Gilderoy Lockhart—a famous wizard who was also the new Defense Against the Dark Arts teacher during Harry's second year.

Professor Lockhart loves to surround himself with his portraits. Find and circle in each small picture a difference from the big picture.

Did you know . . .?

Professor Lockhart won the *Witch Weekly's* Most Charming Smile Award five times in a row.

Professor Lockhart founded the Duelling Club at Hogwarts to show students how to defend themselves when in distress.

Find and circle the other half of the photo to find out who joined Lockhart in the Club's first duel.

Remus Lupin also came to Hogwarts to teach Defense Against the Dark Arts. Sometimes, he was replaced by Professor Snape.

When there's a full moon, Professor Lupin turns into a werewolf. Help him turn back into human form by drawing his portrait.

A former Auror, Alastor Moody, taught Defense Against the Dark Arts during Harry's fourth year.

Professor Moody is called "Mad-Eye" because he has a magic eye that allows him to see who is sticking gum under the bench behind his back. Use the clues to find this student.

The student you are looking for:

- Belongs in Gryffindor.
- Has his or her hands down.
- Doesn't sit in the front row.
- Has short hair.

Did you know . . .?

Legend has it that half of the prisoners at the wizarding prison Azkaban were caught by Professor Moody.

Answer on page 95.

Rubeus Hagrid, the Keeper of Keys and Grounds at Hogwarts, knows almost everything about magical creatures.

Hagrid has always wanted a pet dragon, but they are forbidden. Follow the color pattern below to find where he's hidden a dragon egg.

Did you know . . .?

Hagrid can get along with almost any magical creature, even an Acromantula—a huge spider that can speak!

Answer on page 95.

Students learn about unusual species of magical creatures, their powers, and habits. Hagrid became a professor of these classes during Harry's third year.

Hagrid introduced Buckbeak the Hippogriff in class. Spot five differences between Harry and Buckbeak and their reflection.

Answers on page 95.

The wizarding world is full of amazing creatures. Some are like animals known to Muggles, but they are very dangerous.

Did you know . . .?

According to Hagrid, even the most dangerous magical creatures can become pets.

TEST YOUR KNOWLEDGE

Find out if you know as much about magical creatures as Hagrid.

You will find the answers to all questions in this book.

1

What does an Acromantula look like?

1. Like a big dog
2. Like a big spider
3. Like a big cat

2

How many heads does Fluffy, the huge dog guarding the Sorcerer's Stone, have?

1. Two
2. Three
3. Four

3

What is the name of the giant serpent hidden in the Chamber of Secrets?

1. A Mandrake
2. A centaur
3. A Basilisk

4

Is possessing a dragon allowed at Hogwarts?

1. Yes
2. No
3. Yes, but only on the third floor of the castle.

5

What kind of creature is Buckbeak?

1. A Hippogriff
2. A Thestral
3. A dragon

Check the correct answers on page 95 and see what your magical zoo would look like.

1–2 correct answers

Maybe consider one small but special magical creature.

3–4 correct answers

You would be a great keeper for a little magical herd.

5 correct answers

You could be surrounded by tons of magical creatures. Even the more dangerous ones.

Answers on page 95.

Sybill Trelawney teaches Divination. Students have witnessed her dark predictions, but most of them never come true.

Professor Trelawney reads palms as well. Find and circle the path with the most crystal balls to see whose palm she will read next. Write the correct letters in the spaces below!

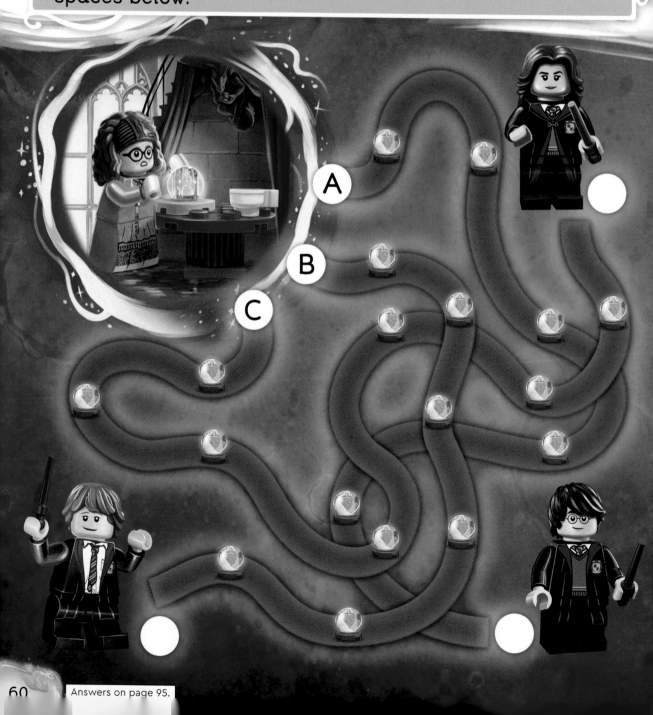

Answers on page 95.

During class, students learn how to predict the future through crystal-ball gazing, palm reading, and even tea-leaf reading.

Where are all the cups with used tea leaves? Count the cups hidden in the picture and write the total in the box below.

Did you know...?

Hogwarts students don't take Divination until their third year.

Answer on page 95.

Students from the Beauxbatons Academy of Magic and the Durmstrang Institute joined Hogwarts for the Triwizard Tournament.

Draw arrows from each fragment to complete the crests of the schools visiting Hogwarts.

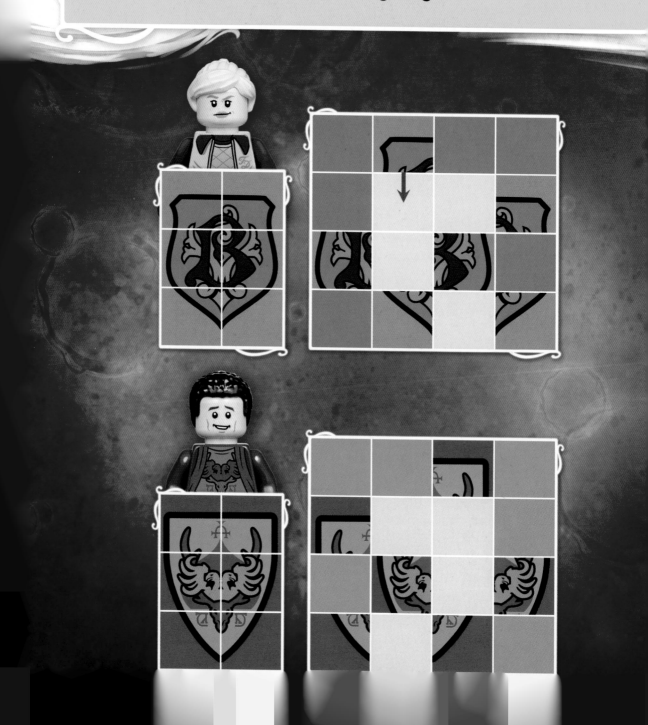

To take part in the tournament, students throw their name into the Goblet of Fire. One champion from each school is chosen.

The Goblet of Fire has chosen a fourth contestant! Find the color code that is identical to the one in the Goblet of Fire to find out who it is.

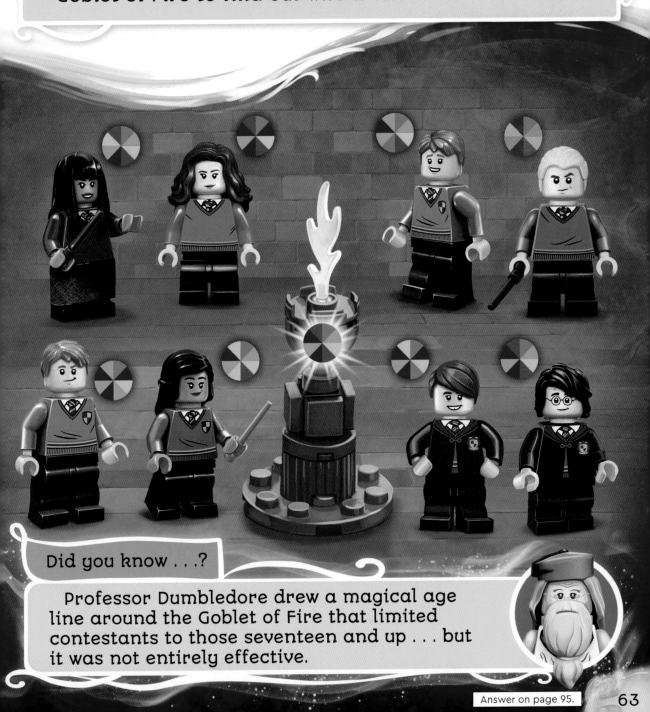

Did you know . . .?

Professor Dumbledore drew a magical age line around the Goblet of Fire that limited contestants to those seventeen and up . . . but it was not entirely effective.

Answer on page 95.

The Goblet of Fire chose Fleur Delacour from Beauxbatons, Victor Krum from Durmstrang, and Cedric Diggory and Harry Potter from Hogwarts.

Find the photo that matches the one of the Tournament participants that was printed in *the Daily Prophet*.

Did you know . . .?

Viktor Krum is a professional Quidditch player who is one of the best Seekers in the world.

Answer on page 95.

The Triwizard Tournament consists of three tasks: getting a golden egg guarded by a dragon, freeing friends from the bottom of the lake, and surviving a dangerous maze.

Lead the contestants through the winding paths of the maze to find out who finds the Cup.

Answers on page 96.

The Yule Ball was held during the Triwizard Tournament. Students had to wear formal clothes and master official dance routines.

Ron's mom sent him traditional dress robes. Check off his correct mirror image.

Answer on page 96.

The Ball begins with a dance by the tournament participants and their companions. They are quickly joined by others.

Almost everyone had a great time at the Ball. Look around the dance floor and circle who's missing.

Did you know . . .?

The Weird Sisters, one of the most beloved bands in the wizarding world, played at the Ball.

Answers on page 96.

In their third year, students can visit Hogsmeade—a wizarding village near Hogwarts. These outings take place on weekends.

Visit Honeydukes and write the numbers of the missing pieces in the empty boxes below to complete the picture.

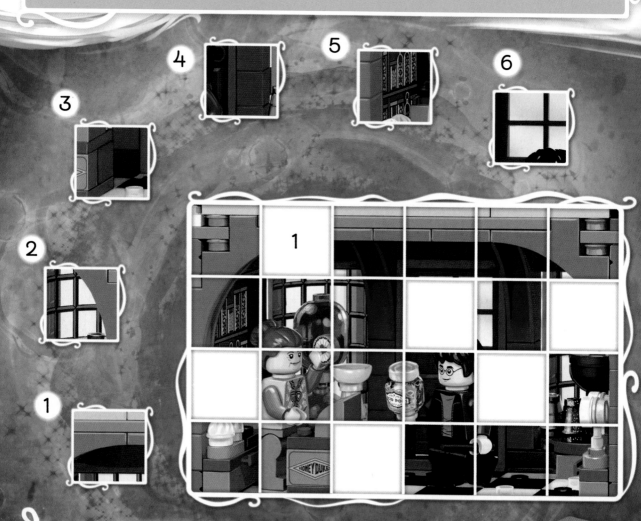

Did you know . . .?

Only students who have a signed permission slip may participate in Hogsmeade visits.

HOGSMEADE

Answers on page 96.

Students and teachers love to visit the Three Broomsticks Inn. It's a small pub in Hogsmeade run by Madame Rosmerta.

Find and circle a student not standing in front of the inn—they've snuck into a secret meeting for adult wizards only.

Answer on page 96.

There are no classes during the holidays. Most students go home for Christmas break, but some stay at Hogwarts.

Harry spent one of his Christmas breaks in London. Fill in the numbers of the missing portraits in each section to see all the people he celebrated with.

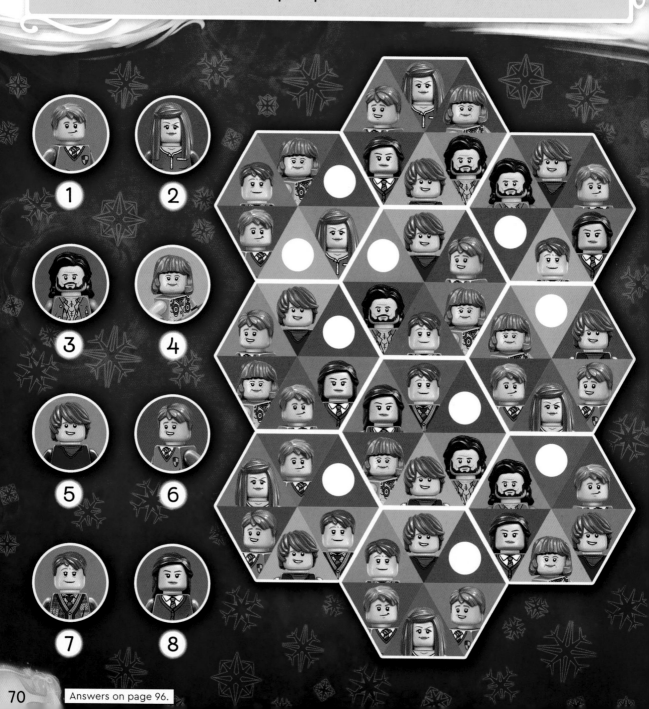

1

2

3

4

5

6

7

8

Answers on page 96.

Hogwarts during Christmas looks even more magical. There are Christmas trees, decorations, and even ghost carolers.

Find and circle the box that is not covered by the others—it contains the Cloak of Invisibility.

Did you know . . .?

On Christmas morning, students who stayed in school for holidays run down to their common rooms where gifts await.

Answer on page 96.

The area surrounding Hogwarts is just as amazing. There is a Whomping Willow that attacks anyone who comes close to it.

Connect the dots and find out what this dangerous tree looks like.

Did you know . . .?

The Whomping Willow hides a secret passage way to the Shrieking Shack—the most haunted place in Britain.

Answer on page 96.

Apart from Care of Magical Creatures classes, Hogwarts students are not allowed to enter the forest near the school.

Help Harry and Ron on their important mission. Follow the spider shown in the blue box to find the right path.

START

FINISH

Answer on page 96.

Shortly after Dolores Umbridge became the new Defense Against the Dark Arts teacher, the Ministry of Magic made her the High Inquisitor of Hogwarts.

As High Inquisitor, Professor Umbridge assessed other teachers. The one that appears on her list the most times gets the lowest rating. Find this teacher by writing the totals for each in the empty boxes below.

Did you know . . .?

Professor Umbridge decorated her office with a collection of plates with cats that moved and meowed.

Answers on page 96.

For several months, Dolores Umbridge replaced Professor Dumbledore as headmistress and made several new rules.

Who was fed up with the new headmistress and quit school? Fill in the pattern of dominoes and find the students in the red boxes to find out.

One of the most unusual chambers at Hogwarts, the Room of Requirement only appears when someone truly needs it.

Neville found the entrance to the Room of Requirement. Connect the dots of the coordinates below to find the magic door.

A2 → B1 → C1 → D2 → D4 → A4 → A2

	A	B	C	D
1	○	○	○	○
2	○	○	○	○
3	○	○	○	○
4	○	○	○	○

Did you know . . .?

The Room of Requirement transforms itself into whatever the witch or wizard needs it to be at a given moment in time.

Answer on page 96.

Harry and his friends formed Dumbledore's Army—a group who wanted to prepare for Lord Voldemort's return.

Students of three houses joined Dumbledore's Army. Look at the colors of the members' uniforms and circle the missing house crest.

DUMBLEDORE'S ARMY

Hermione Granger
Ron Weasley
Harry Potter
George Weasley
Fred Weasley
Ginny Weasley
Luna Lovegood
Neville Longbottom

RAVENCLAW

SLYTHERIN

GRYFFINDOR

HUFFLEPUFF

Answer on page 96.

Dolores Umbridge banned school clubs, so Dumbledore's Army meetings were secretly held in the Room of Requirement.

Learn about the magic spells Dumbledore's Army practiced by matching the bubbles with the same shape.

1 Reducto

2 Expelliarmus

3 Stupefy

4 Expecto Patronum

Answers on page 96.

Professor Umbridge wanted to know what Harry and his friends were up to, so Filch and a few students helped her patrol Hogwarts.

See what these patrols looked like. Figure out the pattern and write the numbers of Umbridge's favorite squad in the blank spaces.

Did you know . . .?

Professor Umbridge issued a lot of Educational Decrees, which are do's and don'ts for Hogwarts students.

PROCLAMATION N°23

DOLORES UMBRIDGE HAS BEEN APPOINTED HIGH INQUISITOR

Answers on page 96.

This is a charm that can protect you from Dementors. It usually takes the form of a guardian animal.

Did you know . . .?

The shape of a Patronus reflects the spellcaster's personality. Harry Potter's Patronus was a stag, like his father.

TEST YOUR KNOWLEDGE
How much do you know about Patronuses?

1

Which charm should you use to cast a Patronus?

Hint: It includes a word similar to the word "Patronus."

1. *Bombarda Maxima!*
2. *Expecto Patronum!*
3. *Everte Statuom!*
4. *Partis Temporus!*

2

A Patronus is a form of positive energy materialized as . . .

Hint: The number of Harry Potter's close friends.

1. A lightning bolt
2. Silvery-white mist
3. Nothing invisible
4. The mirror image of the spellcaster

3

What must you be when casting a Patronus?

Hint: The number of people living in the Dursleys' house when Harry left for Hogwarts.

1. In a good mood
2. Very determined
3. Recalling your happiest memory
4. Ready for a fight

4 What form does Hermione's Patronus take?

Hint: The number of trophies awarded at the Triwizard Tournament.

1. An otter
2. A stag
3. A cat
4. A doe

5 Dumbledore's Army practiced casting Patronus spells in . . .

Hint: It is a room that is there when you need it.

1. The Room of Requirement
2. Hogwarts' Library
3. The Restricted Section
4. The Chamber of Secrets

Check your answers on page 96. If you had the correct answer to:

1-2 questions

Not bad! But you still need to uncover some secrets.

3-4 questions

Great! You know almost everything about Patronuses!

5 questions

Congratulations! You're an expert on Patronuses! Keep up the good work!

Horace Slughorn taught Potions to Harry's parents. He came out of retirement to teach during Harry's sixth year at the request of Professor Dumbledore.

Untangle the lines and see who won Professor Slughorn's Draught of Living Death competition.

Did you know . . .?

Professor Slughorn collects pictures of his former students who became famous. Among them there is the captain of the Holyhead Harpies, Gwenog Jones.

Answer on page 96.

Harry found an old Potions textbook full of useful notes that was marked as property of the Half-Blood Prince.

Harry often looked to his Potions textbook. Find this mysterious book in each picture.

Horace Slughorn sent invitations to the Slug Club to the most talented students and those from famous wizarding families.

Who did not receive an invitation to the Club? Find four identical portraits connected to each other to find out.

Answer on page 96.

Professor Slughorn plans fancy dinners and parties for the members of his Club.

Elegant clothes are required at Slug Club parties. Match the students' outfits to the zoomed-in images.

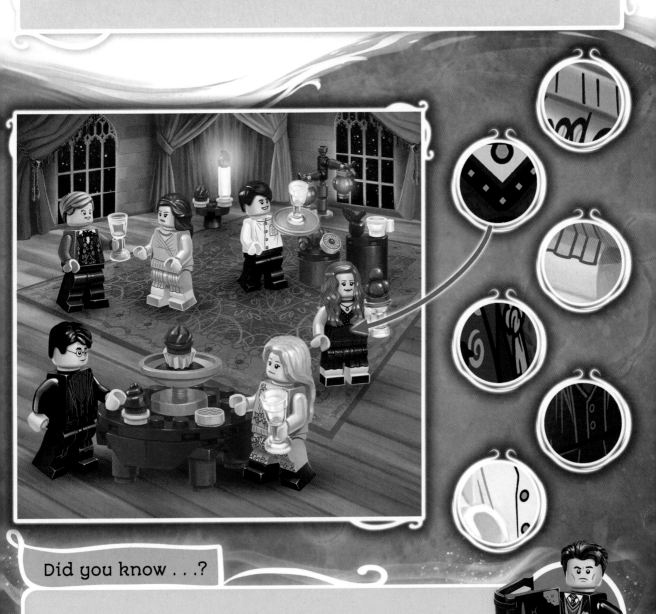

Did you know . . .?

Years ago, Tom Riddle, later known as Lord Voldemort, was a member of the Slug Club.

Answers on page 96.

Hogwarts students may bring one animal to school—an owl, a cat, or a toad. Ron is an exception—he took the rat, Scabbers, with him.

Hermione's cat and Ron's rat are chasing each other! Circle the animal in each row that is running in a different direction than the rest.

Answers on page 96.

Lots of ghosts live at Hogwarts. School ghosts can be found in the corridors, in the Great Hall, and even in bathrooms.

Meet the Gryffindor ghost—Nearly Headless Nick. Number the portraits of Sir Nicholas, starting from the picture where he is least visible to the one where you can see him best.

Did you know . . .?

Other houses have their own ghosts too—the Bloody Baron, the Grey Lady, and the Fat Friar.

Answers on page 96.

To celebrate the successes of their house, Hogwarts students throw parties in their common room.

See what the Quidditch Cup trophy looks like by coloring the squares marked with the letter Q yellow.

H	H	H	G	G	G	S	S	S	S
H	H	G	Q	Q	Q	Q	S	R	S
H	Q	Q	Q	Q	Q	Q	Q	Q	R
H	Q	G	Q	Q	Q	Q	G	Q	R
S	Q	Q	Q	Q	Q	Q	Q	Q	R
S	G	G	Q	Q	Q	Q	G	G	G
S	H	G	H	Q	Q	G	G	S	S
S	H	H	H	Q	Q	S	S	S	R
R	R	R	Q	Q	Q	Q	G	R	R
R	R	R	G	G	G	G	R	R	H

Did you know . . .?

During the Triwizard Tournament, Gryffindor students threw a party in honor of Harry.

Answer on page 96.

Many relationships were born within the walls of Hogwarts. It was at school that Harry's parents, Lily and James, met.

And who was Harry's first school crush? Find and circle the character that appears in all four groups.

Answer on page 96.

Harry didn't like holidays with Aunt Petunia, Uncle Vernon, and their son Dudley. He preferred the company of his friends.

This is the Dursleys house where Harry spent most of his summer holidays. Outline the small pictures that appear on the large picture.

Answers on page 96.

Harry spent a few summer breaks with the Weasley family in their unusual home called The Burrow.

Where have all the Weasleys gone? Find and circle all the characters shown in the box in the picture.

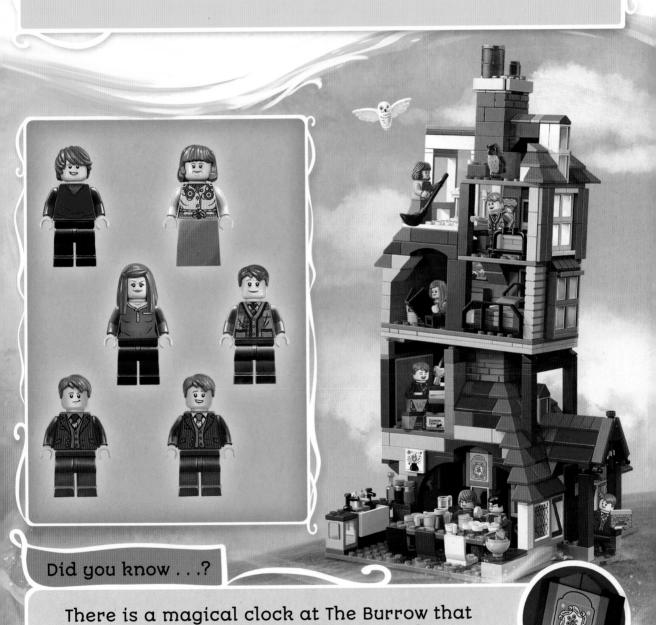

Did you know . . .?

There is a magical clock at The Burrow that shows where each member of the Weasley family is at any given moment.

Answers on page 96.

There are special exams at Hogwarts at the end of the school year. For the first four years, there are exams for each subject.

Did you know . . .?

O.W.L., or Ordinary Wizarding Level, is the exam taken by fifth year students. N.E.W.T., or the Nastily Exhausting Wizarding Test, is taken by the seventh year students.

TEST YOUR KNOWLEDGE
Feel like a Hogwarts student? Take the test and see how much you know about this magical school.

You will find the answers to all questions in this book.

1

On which birthday do students learn that they have been accepted to Hogwarts?

1. 9th
2. 10th
3. 11th
4. 12th

HOGWARTS

2

When does the Hogwarts Express leave for Hogwarts?

LONDON TO HOGWARTS
Platform 9¾

1. August 31, at 11:00 a.m.
2. September 1, at 11:00 a.m.
3. August 31, at 12:00 p.m.
4. September 1, at 12:00 p.m.

3

Which animal is in the crest of Hufflepuff?

1. A badger
2. A snake
3. A lion
4. An eagle

HUFFLEPUFF

4

What is the name of
Mr. Filch's cat?

1. Fluffy
2. Mrs. Norris
3. Norbert
4. Crookshanks

5

Who referees school
Quidditch matches?

1. Professor Snape
2. Professor McGonagall
3. Madam Hooch
4. Hagrid

6

What is the name of the
Triwizard Tournament's
traditional ball?

1. The Valentine's Day Ball
2. The Easter Ball
3. The Halloween Ball
4. The Yule Ball

Check the correct answers on page 96 and
check your level of knowledge about Hogwarts.

1–2 correct
answers

ACCEPTABLE—Hogwarts has
a few more mysteries for you.

3–4 correct
answers

EXCEEDS EXPECTATIONS—you know
almost everything about Hogwarts!

5–6 correct
answers

OUTSTANDING—you know as much
about Hogwarts as Hermione, which
is . . . everything!

Answers on page 96.

ANSWERS

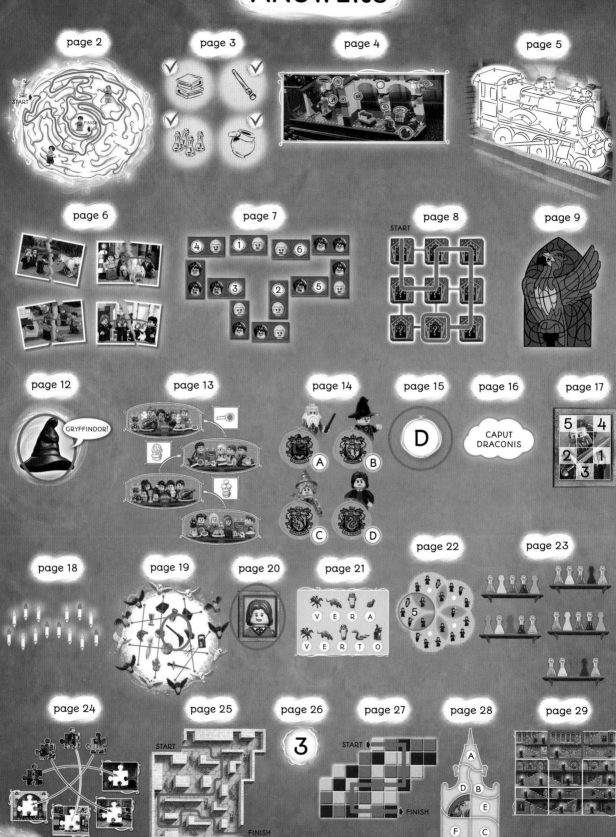

page 2

page 3

page 4

page 5

page 6

page 7

page 8

page 9

page 12

GRYFFINDOR!

page 13

page 14

A B C D

page 15

D

page 16

CAPUT DRACONIS

page 17

5 4 2 1 3

page 18

page 19

page 20

page 21

V E R A

V E R T O

page 22

5

page 23

page 24

page 25

START

FINISH

page 26

3

page 27

START

FINISH

page 28

A

D B

E

F C

page 29

page 30

page 31

page 32

page 33

page 34

page 35

page 36

page 37

page 38

1.3
2.3
3.1

page 39

4.4
5.2

page 40

page 41

page 42

page 43

page 44

page 45

page 46

page 47

page 48

page 49

page 50

1.1
2.2
3.2

page 51

4.3
5.1

page 52

page 53

page 55

page 56

page 57

page 58

1.2
2.2
3.3

page 59

4.2
5.1

page 60

page 61

page 62

page 63

page 64

page 65

page 66

page 67

page 68

page 69

page 70

page 71

page 72

page 73

page 74

7

page 75

page 76

page 77

page 78

page 79

page 80

1.2
2.2
3.3

page 81

4.1
5.1

page 82

page 83

page 84

page 85

page 86

page 87

page 88

page 89

page 90

page 91

page 92

1.3
2.2
3.1

page 93

4.2
5.3
6.4